LOST TALES

Stories for the Tsar's Children

GLEB BOTKIN

VILLARD
NEW YORK

All rights reserved under International and Pan-American Copyright Conventions.
Published in the United States by Villard Books, a division of Random House, Inc.,
New York, and simultaneously in Canada by Random House
of Canada Limited, Toronto.

VILLARD BOOKS is a registered trademark of Random House, Inc.

Some photographs have been previously published.

ISBN 0-679-45142-0

Random House website address: http://www.randomhouse.com/

Printed in the United States of America on acid-free paper

24689753

FIRST EDITION

Book design by Carole Lowenstein

One afternoon in early September 1911, a young brother and sister boarded the Russian Imperial yacht *Standart* as it lay at anchor in the gentle waters of the Crimea. Gleb Botkin, eleven, and his thirteen-year-old sister, Tatiana, had come to visit their father, Dr. Eugene Botkin, personal physician to the Imperial family, who was confined to his cabin with an injury. (He had fractured his kneecap while rushing to aid his friend Peter Stolypin, the prime minister, who had just been struck by an assassin's bullets.) Over a period of eleven days Gleb and Tatiana met face to face not only Tsar Nicholas II and Empress Alexandra but also the five Imperial children. Beneath the white canvas awnings that covered the yacht's gleaming decks, they made the personal acquaintance of Grand Duchesses Olga, Tatiana, Marie, and Anastasia and the heir to the throne, Tsarevich Alexis.

Olga and Tatiana, at sixteen and fourteen years of age, were rapidly ap-

Grand Duchesses Marie, Tatiana, Olga, and Anastasia, Empress Alexandra Feodorovna and Tsar Nicholas II, and Tsarevich Alexis, 1913

proaching young womanhood, but twelve-year-old Marie and ten-year-old Anastasia, along with their seven-year-old brother, were of an age to find much in common with the doctor's handsome son and pretty daughter. The encounter reinforced an earlier friendly mutual interest that lasted until the murders at Ekaterinburg and afforded Gleb and his sister intimate knowledge of much that ultimately culminated in one of the most dramatic and tragic episodes of the twentieth century.

The Botkins were a distinguished family who had served at the Russian court for many years. Court positions brought prestige and respect, but rarely did they encompass intimacy with the Imperial family. With his warm manner, honesty, and unflinching devotion, however, Dr. Eugene Botkin, like his famous father, Dr. Sergei Botkin (court physician to Tsars Alexander II and Alexander III), had become a favorite of the ruling Romanovs. Gleb and Tatiana shared their father's respect and love for the Imperial family, who lived in secluded splendor at Tsarskoe Selo.

Tsar Nicholas II, Dr. Eugene Botkin, and Captain Alexander Drentelin, the tsar's aide-de-camp, 1909

The rarefied world of palaces, yachts, and bowing courtiers in which they were raised isolated the Imperial children from ordinary, everyday life. For the grand duchesses and the tsarevich, the children of their beloved Dr. Botkin provided an endlessly fascinating glimpse into the universe beyond the palace walls. The young Romanovs plied the doctor with questions about Gleb and Tatiana and their brothers; and the doctor's children were equally eager to learn all that protocol permitted their father to tell them of daily life at the court. Gleb had a talent for art, and his sketches and stories had entertained and amused the Imperial children for several years. Gifted with a strong sense of humor and the ability to translate his high-spirited view of the world to paper, Gleb drew and painted animals exuding personality, many of them elegantly attired in military or court uniforms complete with shining medals and decorations.

To most Russians, the children of the tsar must have seemed sheltered and unapproachable—seen only across a dusty parade ground or gazing serenely from a postcard. But Gleb came to know the hearts and souls behind these public images: Tsarevich Alexis, a sensitive boy who longed for good health and unrestrained freedom; Marie, whose cheerful manner perfectly matched her stunning beauty; and, of course, Anastasia, renowned for her tomboy antics and feared for her biting wit.

Grand Duchesses Marie, Tatiana, Anastasia, and Olga, 1914

In 1913 the Romanov dynasty celebrated three hundred years of rule. As the tsar and his family visited cities and monasteries across Russia, they were greeted with deafening cheers. Their empire seemed secure. But these peaceful scenes were not to last. Within four years a revolution would sweep the tsar from his throne, forever changing the lives of both the Imperial family and the Botkins.

In early March 1917, as the monarchy found itself beset by the pressures of wartime demands and the deficiencies of its administrative structures, a number of generals and a group of members of the Duma (the Russian parliamentary body) persuaded Tsar Nicholas II to abidicate his throne. Thus ended the long rule of the Romanov dynasty. Chaos ensued, with the newly formed, so-called Provisional Government no more able to govern effectively than had been the monarchy it replaced.

At the time of the abdication, the tsar and his family were placed under house arrest in the neoclassical Alexander Palace in Tsarskoe Selo, the imperial enclave fifteen miles south of Petrograd. Then, in August 1917, on orders from Alexander Kerensky, the prime minister of the Provisional Government, the family was moved to the Siberian town of Tobolsk, ostensibly to distance them from the disorderly Petrograd mobs. The quiet provincial town was to be the Romanovs' abode for the next eight months.

Unlike so many of the thousands of uniformed and glamorous courtiers who had surrounded Nicholas and Alexandra, Dr. Botkin did not abandon the Romanovs after the February Revolution. He remained attached to the family as their personal physician, trying to ignore the very real dangers his loyalty could bring to him and to his own children. In Tobolsk the Romanovs were housed in a former governor's mansion; Dr. Botkin was given rooms

The deposed tsar with his son, Alexis, in Tobolsk

across the street in a house that had belonged to a wealthy merchant named Kornilov.

Dr. Botkin was one of the few to whom daily access to the Governor's House was permitted. Security tightened even further after a friend of Grand Duchess Olga arrived in Tobolsk on her own and was suspected by the revolutionary guards of being a spy sent by monarchist sympathizers. Upon joining their father, Tatiana and Gleb were denied passes for entry to the Governor's House, and the empress's request that they be permitted to join the Imperial children in their studies was refused. (Sharing Christmas at the Governor's House was also to be forbidden to Dr. Botkin's children.)

The Imperial family was confined to a small, makeshift yard enclosed by a high stockade fence and patrolled by heavily armed guards. It was against this background—the period of the Provisional Government, before the effects of the Bolshevik coup of October 1917 could be felt—that Gleb created the pictures and stories of Mishka Toptiginsky that are reproduced in these albums. Taking advantage of his daily visits to the Governor's House, Dr. Botkin began secretly carrying Gleb's work back and forth between his son and the Imperial children.

These albums, perhaps reminders of happier, carefree days, must have brightened the children's lives. The stories, about revolutionaries seizing control of a monkey kingdom and the efforts of a twelve-year-old bear to restore an imprisoned monarch to his throne, surely captivated the young Romanovs. Gleb managed to introduce a good deal of humor into his detailed

Gleb Botkin, c. 1920–22

paintings and imaginative story lines. As uncertainty in the children's lives increased, these tales and illustrations must have spoken to them of the world they had lost and of happier times they hoped would come.

In November 1917 news filtered out to Tobolsk of the coup in the capital led by Lenin and his Bolsheviks. Within six months the Imperial family found themselves transferred abruptly to the Ural Mountains mining town of Ekaterinburg, a center of Bolshevik power in the burgeoning civil war. In a decision that must have torn at the hearts of both families, Dr. Botkin left behind his own children and accompanied the prisoners into the unknown.

In July 1918, in the basement of the Ipatiev House, an Ekaterinburg residence, the tsar and members of his family, together with Dr. Botkin and three loyal retainers, were brutally murdered on Lenin's orders.

The seventeen-year-old boy who spent hours hunched over a desk before his sketch pad had no idea that his work would become part of his legacy to history. The albums created in Tobolsk as a distraction for the isolated and anxious Imperial children have since been infused with unforeseen human and historic value by the dramatic ending of the Russian empire and the tragedy of the Romanovs. Now, from across the decades, Gleb Botkin's stories and paintings evoke a vanished era and provide a poignant glimpse into one of the last pleasures enjoyed by the Romanov children.

—*Greg King*

ACKNOWLEDGMENTS

Prime thanks go to Dr. Ronald C. Moe and Grace Moe, who conceived this project, and to Mary Matalin, who took the first steps toward its realization.

Many thanks to Villard publisher David Rosenthal, who recognized the uniqueness of the work and saw purpose in its publication. Jennifer Webb was my lifeline to David and offered significant assistance. My thanks also to copy editor Susan M. S. Brown, production manager Leta Evanthes, and production editor Benjamin Dreyer.

I feel extremely indebted to Greg King, who undertook the writing of the foreword.

I owe special thanks to Robert B. Barnett, Esq., for his patient legal counsel.

Deep appreciation is due Masha Tolstoya Sarandinaki, who in the midst of moving house and family managed to perform the time-consuming task of translating the original Russian text.

Thanks go also to my son-in-law Major Charles E. Dean, who reviewed the military insignia and titles; to Zoja Peters, who always had solutions to problems that confronted me; and to Gerald B. Nelson, for the excellence of his photographic work and for the exquisite care with which he treated the fragile materials.

I feel special gratitude to Dr. James H. Billington, for his kindness in examining the albums. His enthusiasm confirmed for me the merit of this undertaking.

Huge thanks to my husband, Dick, who took upon himself with great energy and cheerfulness the somewhat unfamiliar role of amanuensis and general factotum.

Finally, I should like to recognize the many others, unknown to me by name, who participated in the processes of publication.

—*Marina Botkin Schweitzer*

CONTENTS

INTRODUCTION

As the daughter of Gleb Botkin, the creator of these albums, I am very happy and proud to welcome their publication. It is difficult for me to realize that it was Empress Alexandra who first suggested publication of my father's earlier drawings almost ninety years ago.

Gleb Botkin began painting his pictures at about eight years of age, shortly before the appointment in 1908 of his father, Dr. Eugene Botkin, to the post of court physician to the Russian Imperial family in Tsarskoe Selo. The Romanov children were familiar with Gleb's animal drawings and had entered into a game of Gleb's invention involving a group of animals inhabiting the planet Mars. The tsarevich, Alexis, and Grand Duchesses Marie and Anastasia enjoyed suggesting stories, asking for specific illustrations, and copying the drawings. (On one occasion, when making a written request to be carried from the palace by my grandfather, Alexis crossed out his signature, explaining that he did not want his request to be taken for an Imperial order.)

In the early fall of 1917, Gleb Botkin joined his father and sister in Tobolsk, where the Imperial family was being held prisoner. In spite of the shortage of art supplies there—my father had few paints and only one rough brush (nicknamed "the broom" by my grandfather)—Gleb continued to create his stories and drawings. The information he printed in the lower-left-hand corners of the original pages of Russian text indicates that he did the work on a close to daily basis in To-

Gleb Botkin, 1917

COURTESY OF MARINA BOTKIN SCHWEITZER

bolsk. (See Chapter XV, p. 35, for an example.)

It is important to understand that the stories accompanying the watercolors were never meant for general readership. They were simply a means of communication and a source of shared amusement among young friends. The episodes were composed hurriedly, and Gleb made no serious attempt to structure the narrative carefully.

The chief value of the text lies in the topics treated and the glimpse they afford into the sentiments and subjects of interest to all the young people involved—internal and international politics, government structures, the power of a subservient and dishonest press, betrayal of common ideals, and the abandonment of traditional values. Also meticulously recorded are the dress, traditions, and pageantry of the military. The four grand duchesses, the tsarevich, and indeed the tsar himself were much taken with the minutiae of proper military attire, and Gleb exercised great care to render his uniforms correct to the smallest detail. (The tsar suffered particularly keenly the order for removal from all uniforms of shoulder boards—symbols of military honor in the Imperial army.)

Gleb's pictures and text are a satire of the events and principals of Russia at the time—the period of Kerensky's Provisional Government (hence, for example, the reference to the "Transitory" government). The sympathies of the Imperial children naturally lying with the advocates of monarchy, it is the monarchist cause that ultimately triumphs over the republican revolutionaries in the story.

These albums constituted one of the few diversions for the Imperial family under the stark conditions of their confinement. Even the tsar had his favorite among the illustrations; he was particularly amused by "the ears of the people" listening to King Kolobok speak from the balcony of his palace. The tsar also sent, through Dr. Botkin, approval for Gleb's original uniform designs.

Dr. Eugene Botkin ultimately shared the fate of his tsar in Ekaterinburg. Gleb Botkin, who together with his sister had been refused permission to follow the Imperial family and his father to Ekaterinburg, made his way to that city immediately upon its fall to the White armies (days after the murders). All evidence in Ekaterinburg pointing to the tragedy there, Gleb returned to Tobolsk and his sister. In March 1919, Gleb and Tatiana traveled to Vladivostok. In the early spring of 1920, the Japanese military, perhaps mindful of Dr. Botkin's humanitarian work at the front during the Russo-Japanese War, enabled Gleb to escape to Japan. There he later retrieved from a friend who had followed him some of the drawings left behind at the time of his precipitate departure.

After marriage in Japan to a young widow, Nadejda Konshin Mandragy, the daughter of a former president of the Russian Bank of State, Gleb and his small family traveled in 1922 to the United States, where they were to make their permanent home. Tatiana and her family first found refuge in Yugoslavia and later established residence in France.

Gleb Botkin disclaimed any artistic merit for his illustrations and referred to them as "just funny drawings." To me, his daughter, they stand for a great deal more. I think of the brave young man, seventeen years of age, who did not hesitate to join his father and the Imperial family in Siberia. I wonder how, in the midst of the horrors of the revolution, with his own life and the lives of those he held most dear in constant peril, he was able to summon the state of mind and power of concentration to compose, day after day, the light-hearted drawings and texts for his stories of the animal tsardom.

Of course, such questions did not occur to me during my childhood. The illustrated adventures of Mishka Toptiginsky were just another commonplace in our somewhat uncommon household. It was only with time's passage that I came to recognize the human and moral values implicit in the creation of this work, values my father steadfastly maintained throughout his life.

Following are brief summaries of the three stories in the album, included for the benefit of readers who might become confused by the many seeming convolutions of the narrative.

It is to be noted that all Russian teddy bears are referred to as "Mishka" (a diminutive of the name Michael). Hence the large number of characters with the name Mishka or some variation thereof.

Part I
Chapters I–XII

Mishka I, King of Mishkoslavia (a Bear kingdom), emerges the victor in a long war (1914–17) against the Monkey Kingdom. Meanwhile, in the Monkey Kingdom, the death of the king (Ludwig XXV) and the capture and imprisonment by the Mishkoslavians of Albert IX, the legitimate heir to Ludwig XXV, present an opportunity for Monkey revolutionaries to overthrow the Monkey monarchy. The Monkey revolutionists set up a provisional ("Transitory") government, which extends to New Littletown, a city located in a frontier territory to which the participants in a failed rebellion of Bears against the Monkey king in 1895 had been exiled.

Mishka Toptiginsky, a twelve-year-old Bear resident of New Littletown and a staunch monarchist, persuades the exiled Bear rebels of 1895 of the error of their ways in having risen against a legitimate monarch, even a Monkey monarch, and rallies them to a counterrevolution against the Monkey revolutionaries.

Part II
Chapters XIII–XXIV

Mishka I, the Bear king of Mishkoslavia, fearing a resumption of hostilities with possible disastrous results for Mishkoslavia if the Monkey monarchy is restored—he had been able to defeat the Monkeys only through treacherous means—gives aid to the Monkey revolutionaries. It is his belief that the establishment of a republic in Monkeyland, with its attendant dissensions, would keep the Monkeys weak and unable to mount another military campaign. Mishka I therefore refuses all aid to Mishka Toptiginsky's royalist cause and proposes to use military force to prevent Mishka Toptiginsky from subduing the Monkey revolutionaries.

However, Mishka Toptiginsky is able to secure sufficient aid from other European monarchs—first, to free the members of the Monkey royal family who were being held by the Mishkoslavians, and then, after numerous military victories over the revolutionaries, to enter the capital of Monkeyland (Paris) in triumph together with the legitimate king of Monkeyland, Albert IX.

Finch Island Episode

The Finch Island episode describes the restoration of monarchy to Finch Island—formerly a dependency of Monkeyland; now, after the defeat of the Monkeys by the Mishkoslavian Bears, a Mishkoslavian protectorate. An account is given of the vacationing King Mishka of Mishkoslavia's visit, with his extended family and retinue, to Finch Island.

—*Marina Botkin Schweitzer*

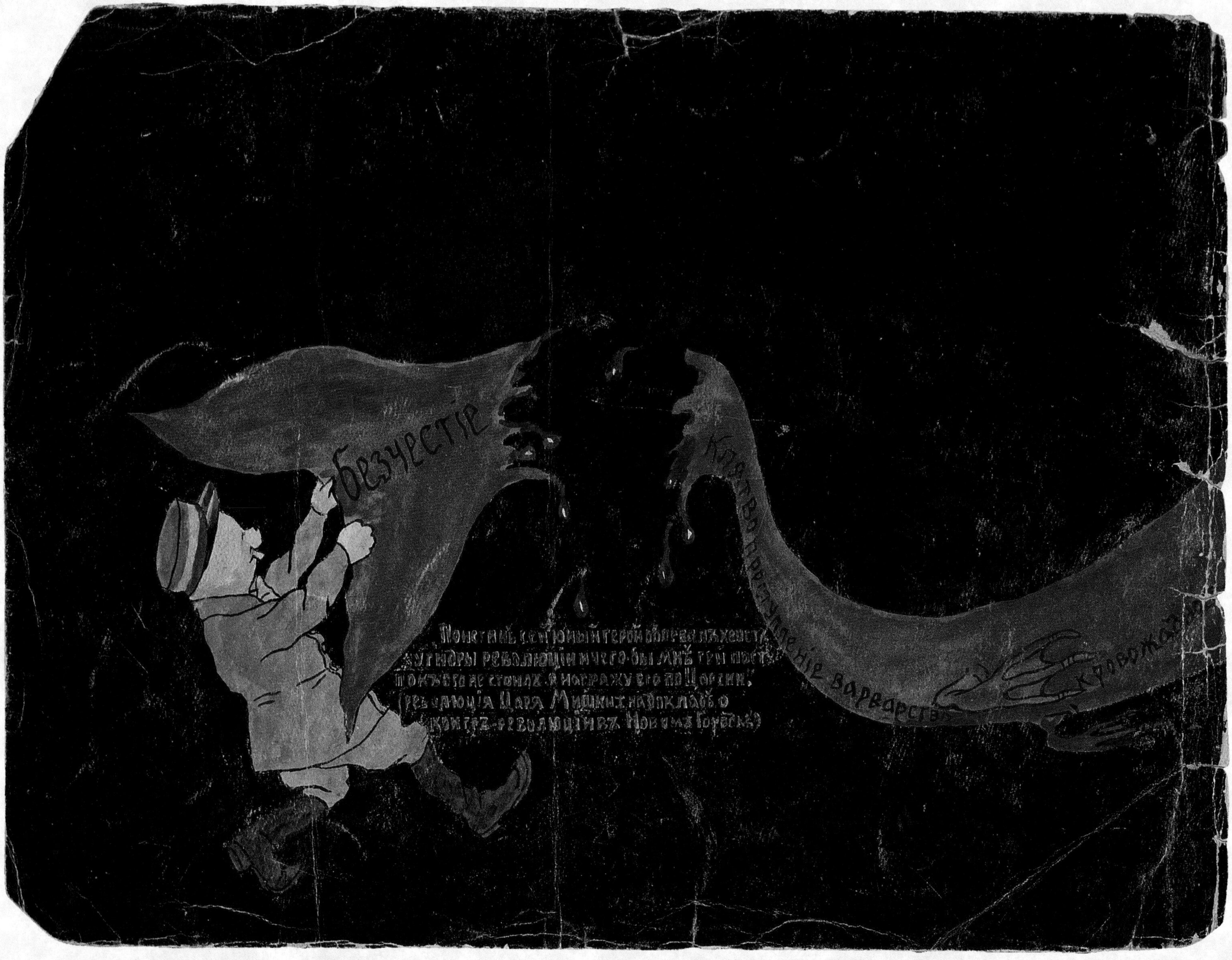

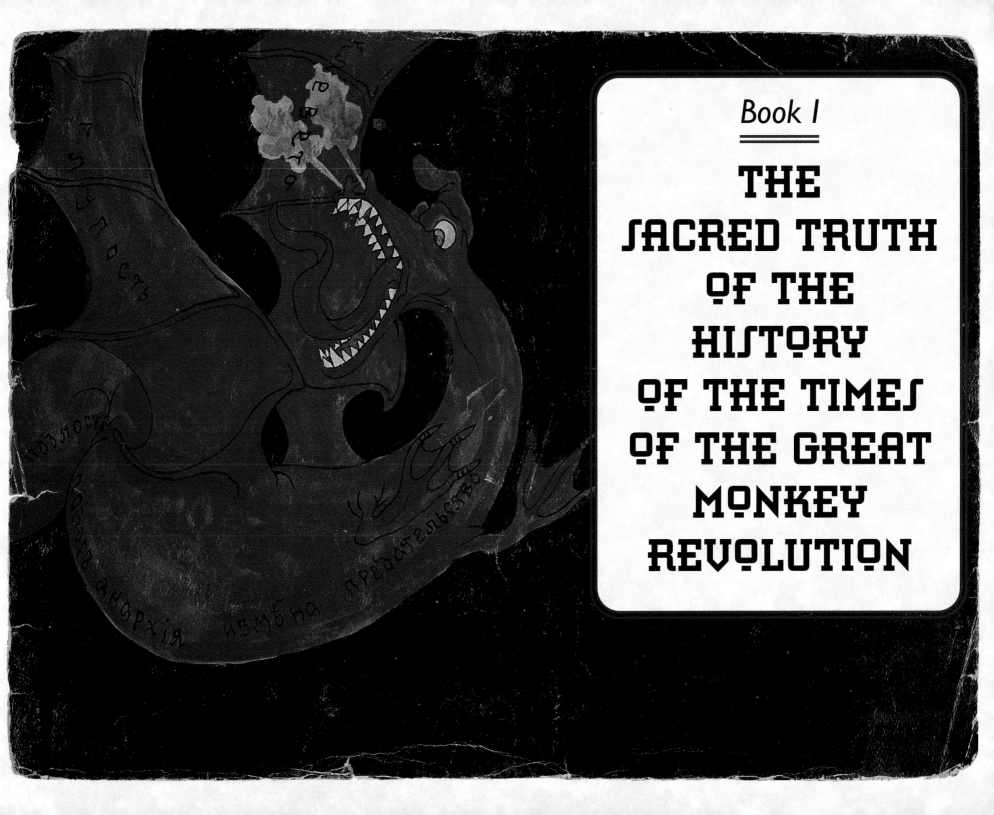

Book I

THE SACRED TRUTH OF THE HISTORY OF THE TIMES OF THE GREAT MONKEY REVOLUTION

Part I

MISHKA PUSHKOVICH TOPTIGINSKY

CHAPTER I

In the year 1895, in the Kingdom of the Monkeys, there suddenly erupted an uprising of the Bears led by a committee from Littletown. The uprising was crushed with exceptional severity, and the inhabitants of Littletown were deported to the easternmost edge of the kingdom's frontier, where they founded New Littletown. However, even there the persecution did not end. New Littletown was put under such economic pressures that despite their prodigious effort and the extraordinary richness of the soil, the inhabitants were barely able to earn enough for a crust of bread. By the year 1917, New Littletown presented a gloomy aspect of desolation and poverty. Moreover, the Monkeys established their own quarter in the town, and, in no time at all, they had completely confused the Bears, selling on credit and lending money with interest. Soon the Monkey quarter became a breeding ground for all sorts of trouble and filth—physical as well as moral.

In that very town there dwelt a hereditary nobleman, Pushok Pushkovich Toptiginsky, with his family. He lived in very poor circumstances; his pride kept him from working for those in the Monkey government who had brought him to ruin. His family consisted of two sons and two daughters.

The oppressive year 1914 dawned—the year of war and horrors. Toptiginsky held out for a long time, but he finally saw that to hang on any longer was impossible. Throwing off all remnants of pride, he accepted the highly lucrative position of Consul for the Monkeys to the Eskimo Husky colonies in Africa. On the first of April 1917, he departed with his family, leaving in town his younger son, the twelve-year-old Mishka, who was studying at the local school and was to move up to Class II in the coming spring. The little bear stood in the road for a long time, waving good-bye with his handkerchief and trying to hold back the sobs rising in his throat. Finally he tore his eyes away, hid the handkerchief in his pocket, and sadly lumbered off to the little room above Kadushka's small store. The room had been rented for Mishka until the end of the school year, when he would be able to join his parents.

But, before we continue our story, it is necessary to explain the political situation on Mars* up to this time.

As is widely known, the Mishkoslavian Tsar, Mishka I, declared war on the Monkeys on July 1, 1914. Both Tsar Mishka and his Prime Minister, Mr. Pig, belonged to the moderate party, and the two forsook their peaceful way of life with great reluctance. But, like the Tsar himself, the Prime Minister was not stupid and preferred to avoid any conflict with the population. Therefore, the two declared war, desiring not to clash with the general population's demand for hostilities, which had been stirred up under pressure from the small but dangerously powerful and desperate military party led by Tsarevich Mishka and Grand Duke Purr. Although Tsar Mishka had declared war, he had not yielded completely, and, despite the clamor from the war party, he entered into friendly negotiations with the Asian Monkeys.

The early part of the war caused the population to lose faith completely in the war party. After a series of awful battles, the shattered Mishkoslavian army retreated, with Tsar Mishka and the Commander in Chief, Grand Duke Purr, holed up in Longridge while the rest of the army was surrounded in Mishkoslavia. Serving in this army, as an ordinary cornet, was the Tsarevich. Realizing that all was lost, he took command, gathered the whole male population, armed them with whatever was at hand, and launched a desperate attack upon the Monkeys. The Monkeys, never expecting resistance, were badly beaten—to the great astonishment of the Tsarevich himself. The Tsarevich made contact with Longridge, and over the summer, together with Grand Duke Purr, rid the entire country of the enemy. As a reward for his heroic feat, the Tsarevich received the rank of colonel, and an independent detachment was placed under his command.

* Although this story takes place on Mars, some cities and towns have names identical to the names of cities and towns on Earth.

Now the war party was still left with the task of provoking war with the Asian Monkeys. However, all attempts were in vain. Then Grand Duke Purr made known his demand for a special army—to undertake an attack deep into enemy territory—with the Tsar himself at its head. Tsar Mishka was delighted and took command, while Premier Pig, who never left the Tsar's side, became Chief of Staff. That is how it became necessary to turn over the running of the country to those next in order of seniority. Tsarevich Mishka was named Regent, and the Minister of Justice, Wagtail, was appointed Premier. The old cabinet resigned, and Wagtail chose a new cabinet exclusively from the ranks of the war party.

A month later, the delegation of Asian Monkeys previously summoned by Tsar Mishka arrived in Mishkoslavia. The Tsarevich-Regent, instead of hosting the prescribed dinner, ordered the delegation out; and war with the Asian Monkeys was achieved.

Tsar Mishka faulted the Premier, but the Tsarevich took all blame upon himself. As punishment he was removed from power and named commander of an infantry regiment. But Wagtail and the entire cabinet stayed in power. Moreover, in time, Wagtail received the full power of Regent, and he began, on the sly, to continue the politics of the Tsarevich. The Tsarevich himself was soon pardoned and named Commander of the Asiatic Army. However, after almost three years of war, the Mishkoslavian Bears began to retreat once again. At a war council, it was decided to risk all on a decisive battle. Every advantage was on the side of the Monkeys, with the exception of one—having received 10 million counterfeit francs from the Bears, the Chief of Staff to Archduke Albert, the Monkey Commander, turned traitor; and the Archduke and his whole army were taken prisoner. Upon hearing this news, old King Ludwig XXV died of a heart attack. In the country shorn of its King and his heir, revolution flared. It is the history of this revolution which is the task of our story.

The revolution had already been long in preparation in the Monkey Kingdom. Considerable—albeit counterfeit—money had been allotted to it, even by Tsar Mishka. But the strict and wise regime of old Ludwig XXV had kept order with a sharp eye, and more than one clever and complicated scheme had been smashed by the vigilant royal police. When the King died, and Archduke Albert, of selfless courage and respected and loved by everyone, was taken prisoner by treacherous means, such a convenient opportunity presented itself that the revolutionaries understood and said: "Now or never." And they attacked.

On the very first day, the revolutionaries crawled into the wine cellars, and the success of the revolution was assured because, by the second day, all of Paris was dead drunk. Robbery, murder, and bestiality ensued. Drunken soldiers were killing officers; workmen were beating soldiers; soldiers and workmen were beating the bourgeoisie; the bourgeoisie, the soldiers, and the workers were slaughtering the aristocrats; complete anarchy began, and everyone understood how very right the Mishkoslavian war party had been to demand war against the Monkeys.

Power in the Monkey Kingdom was divided between the "Transitory Government"* (made up of the bourgeoisie and Parliament) and a "Trade Union of Proletarians at Risk of Being Deprived of Their Freedom." The trade union, leaning on sympathy from the man in the street, was becoming a threat to the government.

The new form of government was met with enthusiasm throughout the country. In celebration, the army, having killed its officers, voluntarily ceded to the Mishkoslavians sixty versts† along the entire frontier. Tsar Mishka sent the Major General of the General Staff, Mishukovsky, to Paris with several billions in counterfeit money to further the best possible outcome for the revolution.

The horrors of the revolution infected even New Littletown. The armed militia stationed there arrested all its own officers and, in spite of the advancing years of its members, set off to plunder the wine cellars in the Monkey quarter. Soon fires, robberies, and gunfire began. But the Bear inhabitants rejoiced and said: "Well, now it is our turn to celebrate. The Monkeys won't be torturing us much longer."

But here, something quite unexpected happened, forcing the inhabitants to turn the course of politics in exactly the opposite direction. The hero of our story, Mishka Toptiginsky, enjoyed great popularity among his contemporaries. A band of forty schoolboys was always ready to serve him, and they had more than once turned the whole school upside-down with their pranks. Now Mishka gathered his band at a rallying point outside the town, and, standing on a hill from which he always gave his speeches, deeply agitated, but speaking in a loud and firm voice and lifting his right paw high, he declaimed:

Our forefathers rose up against the Monkey people who were oppressing them and visited upon themselves the wrath of the Monarch. The sacred hour has come in which the grandsons are given the means to expiate the sins of their forebears. And I, here before you all, solemnly swear—by the sun under which I live, by the air I breathe, by the universe, by all that is to me sacred and great, on my honor and that of my forefathers, by the ghosts of my departed ancestors, by the awful uncertainty awaiting us beyond the city, by all with which I can vow vengeance against the despicable Monkeys for the humbling and desecration of the throne, for the suffering of our ancestors, for the ridicule and debasement of the nobility, for the streams of innocent blood spilled, and for all their countless crimes—I take this awesome and inviolable oath of fidelity to the legitimate Sovereign and King, to Albert IX, seized by treachery; and I declare that nothing and nobody, not even the threat of death, and no matter what suffering, will stop me from fulfilling the many oaths given here, to which I am summoning Heaven itself as a witness.

Who is with me?

"Long live the King! *Vive le roi!* Hurrah! We are all with you!" shouted the youngsters. "We swear it! We will die, but we won't retreat!" The whole crowd rushed after its leader, who was already headed back to the city.

---

* "Transitory" is a play on the word "provisional," as in the term "provisional government." The so-called Provisional Government was in power in Russia at the time this text was being written.

† A verst is 1.06 kilometers, or 3,200 feet.

CHAPTER IV

Mishka led his detachment in the direction of the Monkey quarter, behind which the barracks and weapons and cartridge storehouses were located. They had assumed correctly. The whole revolutionary detachment was looting and drinking in town. Only one half-drunk sentry decked out in red rags had been left behind.

"Hey, you! Snoutface!" shouted Mishka. "Get rid of those red rags right now, and hand your guns over to me."

"In the first place," said the sentry, in a thick-tongued drunken drawl, "be so kind as to speak respectfully to a noble warrior of Free Monkeyland. And, in the second place, I am about to open fire on you, so get out of here!"

"Toozik and Greeneyes, deal with this fine fellow," said Mishka. "You, Bulka and Mishutka, see to this red rag that these scoundrels have hung out here, and the rest of you follow me. We are going to destroy the wine cellars and depots."

Toozik and Greeneyes quickly rendered the sentry harmless. They gathered all his bows, tied him up hand and foot, and laid him down on the grass. Soon, nothing was left of the flag either. The heavy doors of the cellars and depots collapsed rather quickly under the violent charges of the young royalists. The band of boys was quickly transformed into a magnificent armed detachment, equipped with the seized rifles, cartridges, machine guns, machine-gun cartridge belts, revolvers, and swords—in a word, with all the kinds of weapons they had found. Leaving behind two sentries with machine guns to guard what remained in the cellars, depots, and armories, the band went off, under the unquestionable leadership of Mishka, to free the arrested officers.

The captured officers had been put in an empty wooden shed and warned that, at the slightest hint of an attempt to escape, they would be incinerated with the whole shed. In addition, the door was boarded shut from the outside. The shed was left completely unguarded. Mishka ordered the detachment to break down the door. The order was easily executed.

Leaving the detachment outside, Mishka crawled into the shed, bowed low, and, approaching the Colonel, said: "I have the honor to present myself, Hereditary Nobleman Mishka Toptiginsky. Sir, I have come to tender from the entire Bear population its deep apology for permitting the arrest of the gentlemen officers of the royal army by drunken rebels, but I had in all only forty unarmed youngsters under my personal command, and it was impossible for me to enter into a fight with armed insurgents. I had to wait for the moment when the revolutionaries were so distracted by the cult of Bacchus that they left all the arms depots without any protection—if one does not count the drunken sentry with whom we easily dealt. Then, after capturing the weapons, we were able to get to you."

The Colonel grabbed Mishka's paw and shook it for a long time. The officers did not believe their luck. Finally, Mishka began to speak again: "Sir, I have come to the conclusion that without the advantage of machine guns, we shall not be in a position to bring order to the town. Even though I have machine guns and all kinds of arms in abundance, I am fac-ing a significant difficulty in not being able to use machine guns because nobody in my detachment is familiar with them. Therefore, I am taking the liberty of asking one of you gentlemen officers to help us. I, in turn, guarantee that the revolutionary soldiers will not be in a position to take revenge on you. And I promise that, in the course of the next few days, I will have at my disposal not forty youngsters but all the population of the town capable of bearing arms. I vouch that within a week the old regime will be fully reinstated in New Littletown. I agree to give up my life in case of failure. The one thing I ask to enable me to keep my promises is that command be left to me with the stipulation that one of the gentlemen officers will take upon himself the role of technical adviser."

"That I can understand," exclaimed the Colonel. "Mr. Adjutant, you will undertake the execution of the technical side of Mr. Toptiginsky's orders, and we gentlemen officers will deploy as regular officers."

"Yes, sir, Colonel," answered the officers.

Mishka's detachment was immediately brought into proper shape. Each member was armed according to all the rules of the art of warfare. The detachment was formed into a real fighting unit. The officers took their places. Mishka and his adjutant immediately mounted the horses that were brought to them. Toozik was entrusted with a drum, on which he beat cadence brilliantly; and the detachment, to the beat of the drum, with even stride and in step, moved in perfect order to the Monkey quarter.

CHAPTER VI

The soldiers, as has been said, were drinking in the taverns of the Monkey quarter. At the time of Mishka's arrival with his detachment, the valiant revolutionaries were dead drunk. They were firing live cartridges from their rifles, fighting, and engaging in every kind of impropriety. Dispatched at night from a neighboring town, the militia, also not quite sober, tried to induce the combatants, who were running wild, to disperse. Finally, forsaking their intended duties, the militia took up riding solemnly through the town, choosing the quieter spots to be on the safe side.

Approaching the tavern, Mishka ordered his adjutant to surround the vacant plot of land around the town on which the comrades were brawling so that no one could get away. When the directive was carried out, Mishka ordered the capture of a relatively sober comrade and explained to him rather emphatically that all the revolutionaries were to lay down their arms and surrender. When the reluctant bearer of the flag of truce returned to his own side, he was beaten unmercifully, and the rifles were turned upon Mishka.

Then Mishka ordered the tavern set on fire in order to drive out the rioters who were getting drunk inside. It was very easy to burn down the tavern, which had a straw roof and, besides, was full of spirits. When the flames enveloped the building, the revolutionaries ran out in a rage and opened fire on Mishka. In response, the detachment, hidden behind a variety of cover, also opened rifle and machine-gun fire.

Mishka and his adjutant, alone in the whole detachment, did not take cover but rode openly on horseback, observing the field of combat. Had the Monkeys not been so drunk, they would early on have been able to kill them both.

At last, the Monkeys could not withstand the machine-gun fire, and, not seeing the hidden ambush, they rushed to get away, meeting up with bayonets and a barrage of bullets. In about two hours, the drunken soldiers, with their hands tied behind their backs, were installed in barracks where they were locked up and informed that, until their court-martial, they would be held under arrest, and fed only bread and water. Firefighters were ordered to put out the fire. The detachment, on Mishka's orders, went to round up the drunken soldiers and militiamen who were reeling about town. Mishka himself, together with Toozik and Greeneyes, went off to the Governor's Palace to arrest the Commissar of the "Transitory Government," who was making himself at home there. Bulka and five helpers were ordered to free from prison all those who had been arrested by the revolutionaries.

CHAPTER VII

Mishka did not want anyone but himself to have to suffer from the corrupt revolutionary judges in case of a calamity. For that reason, when it was necessary to do anything for which one could later get into trouble, he always acted alone. Thus, he alone was the initiator and inspiration for the counterrevolution. As the leader, he alone could be blamed for the destruction of the wine cellars, since it would be impossible to call a whole crowd of people to account. He alone set the officers free; he alone dared take it upon himself to speak in the name of the Bear populace; and, moreover, he laid on himself alone, in front of the officers, full responsibility in case of failure. And now, going in to see the Commissar, he left his companions outside so that, in case of a mishap, only he would be held to account.

The sentry had drunk so much he had fallen asleep. Mishka had no trouble tying him up and headed through the hall to the Governor's study, where the Commissar sat. At Mishka's entry, the Commissar jumped up and looked with anger and fear at Mishka's huge saber and revolver. "What may I do for you, young man?" asked the Commissar.

"Be so kind as to answer my next question," said Mishka not very politely. "Who are you, anyway?"

"I," cried the Commissar haughtily, "and what kind of stupid Bear are you if you don't know that I am the Commissar of the 'Transitory Government'?"

"A gang of hooligans, charlatans, and swindlers is not a government and cannot have a commissar. If you are a plain agent of a thieving gang, then I am putting you under arrest."

"What gives you so much power?"

"Answer me. What is your name and who are you?"

"Ha! I? I am a respected citizen—if that is more agreeable to you!"

"What? You are a respected citizen of some city or other?"

"What kind of stupid animal are you? I am a citizen of Free Monkeyland, like everyone else, and like you. And who do you think you are?"

"Ah ha!" said Mishka. "And your profession?"

"What kind of question is that? Assistant to the City Attorney. There, is that enough for you? You can clear out now," exclaimed the irritated Commissar.

"But is it clear to you," asked Mishka, "that this house belongs to the state and is intended for the Governor? Whoever you are, because you crept in here and took over, you are a robber, a thief, and a swindler."

"Who do you think you are? I am the Commissar of the 'Transitory Government,' and if you do not clear out of here now, I will call the revolutionary army."

"The revolutionary troops were arrested long ago. I want to spit from the highest height on your 'Transitory Government.' In the name of the King, I declare you arrested, sir. You are to be prosecuted for treason against the King, for violating your oath of allegiance and betraying the country in wartime, for robbery, for infringement of public order, and for appropriating titles not belonging to you. And now be kind enough to follow me, or else . . ." Mishka drew his revolver and held it to the Commissar's temple.

"Woe is me! What bad luck! What kind of horrible people are these? What kind of job did the government give me? What kind of nasty government is it anyway?" moaned the miserable Commissar.

"Fancy talk," barked Mishka as the Commissar cowered and trotted after him. At the gate, Toozik and Greeneyes surrounded the Commissar, tied his hands, and took him away to the barracks.

In the meantime, Bulka freed those who had been arrested. The rest of the detachment rounded up the soldiers and militiamen and restored the police to their old posts. By six o'clock, complete order reigned in the town. Upon Mishka's command, all the red flags were replaced by the national flag. And Mishka, having ordered Toozik to toll the bell for the townspeople to assemble, went off himself to the town hall.

CHAPTER VIII

Since morning, the inhabitants of the Bear quarter had preferred not to venture out of their homes. The shooting that had already begun during the night, the ceremonial entry of the Commissar of the "Transitory Government," the fire in the Monkey quarter, the onset of looting, and the arrival of the militia spread a nervous and fearful mood throughout the town. Moreover, almost all the young boys had run outside to watch the disorders. That made the mothers cry, while the fathers completely lost their senses.

In the middle of the day, rumors spread that the arrested officers were free and that a large number of schoolboys had been present at the riots. These reports further increased the hysteria and augmented the general tension. However, toward five o'clock, the shooting began to abate. The firemen drove by to put out the fire, and when, at about six o'clock, the frightened inhabitants decided to poke their noses out the door, they viewed complete order—not one soldier and not one militiaman. Moreover, a policeman stood on every corner. At the same time, not a single member of Mishka's band had returned, and, for that reason, complete dejection and confusion settled in over the households.

"Well, now, so-o-o-o," drawled the Mayor, Makitka Crosseyes, sitting down to a tasty dinner prepared by his worthy wife, Pinknose. "I don't understand anything. Where did the police come from? Whatever is going on out there, the Monkey Kingdom is falling apart, and we will soon be free. And whoever might have won out there, the republicans or the royalists, just don't let me be Mayor if I have to work for any Monkey whatsoever, no matter how attractively the job may be presented. Do you see, Pinknose, we have lived in poverty because—" The Mayor wanted to begin talking politics, but he suddenly froze, his mouth agape.

From the tower of the town hall resounded an unbelievable clanging, as if instead of one bell there were twenty bells pealing. Toozik had climbed up to the bell tower and, without giving the matter much thought, and with no respect for the age of the bell, began ringing with all his might, repeating, "One, two; one, two; well, let's swing out, old boy— to and fro! You would make a perfect mathematics teacher—a loud voice but a blockhead. Hey, now. One, two; one, two; come on, swing. It's taking them so long to get here, it's obvious our town fathers are completely deaf. Hey, now, old boy, swing out—to and fro—don't be lazy!"

Finally, Greeneyes ran up to say that the town fathers and the whole populace had assembled and that Mishka was about to speak.

Toozik and Greeneyes barely had time to run into the hall since Mishka was already mounting the podium.

"Distinguished Gentlemen," Mishka began in a loud and clear voice, "I have assembled you here for a reason for which I should have preferred not to. My forty young helpers and I have called you together to point out to you that you have forsaken your duty and betrayed your oaths while your children, alone, have fulfilled their duty as *you* ought to have done. Once *you* forsook *your* obligations, it became *our* duty to expiate your failings. I have asked you here not to request, but to demand, that all the populace take up arms and help us. There are only forty of us, and we shall not crush the Monkeys if they should send so much as one division against us.

"Furthermore, until now no one will answer for a single one of my actions except I; and for that reason, if it suits you to continue to act as you have been acting, nobody will touch you. But I will know how to die because I do not want to live to see the further disgrace of my people.

"You don't want to save the King and his government in this moment of peril because he is the *Monkey* King. But, after all, what does it matter whose King he is since you have sworn allegiance to him; or did you swear out of cowardice? But the Commissar who comes here in the name of those holding power over the Monkey people—you can serve him? Watching how the Monkeys are looting your town, you can do that? Tell me straight out, are you those Bear heroes whose fame will not fade as long as Mars exists? If so, stand up for a just cause; if not, if you are just slaves and lackeys to the Monkey people, then acknowledge it openly, and, here, distinguished gentlemen, before all of you, I shall put a bullet through my head because I do not want to survive such a disgrace."

Mishka drew his revolver and fell silent, awaiting an answer.

CHAPTER X

Mishka's speech made a deep impression. First a murmuring began. When it subsided, a deep silence set in. The Mayor opened his mouth in surprise. The Town Councillor bent his head down low. Here and there nervous nose blowing sounded. Finally, an old Bear who lived on a small farm beyond the town, and who was honored and deeply respected for his integrity, intellect, and common sense, stood up, mounted the podium, and said: "Listen, Little Mishka, don't shoot yourself. Why hide our sin? Everyone sees we are guilty, and for that you have given us old men a dressing-down. I don't know about everybody else, but I will follow you wherever you go; and I say that nobody will dare lay a finger on Little Mishka without stepping over the dead body of this old Bear." And the oldster thrice kissed our hero, who was touched to tears.

The thunder of clapping paws was the response to the old Bear, and a booming "Hurrah!" and "Bravo!" shook the town hall. "Distinguished Gentlemen," suddenly shouted Mayor Makitka, "a half hour ago, as I was putting a piece of cutlet in my mouth, I said to my Pinknose: 'I am not going to be Mayor Makitka if I have to work for any Monkey whatsoever.' Now, gentlemen, I solemnly swear that I will remain Mayor Makitka, and I publicly swear fidelity to His Majesty King Albert IX." The mayor raised his right paw. "Earlier, I was just a long-eared fool."

"*Vive le roi!* Hurrah!" yelled the Bears in response.

"Distinguished Gentlemen," the Mayor spoke up again, "I propose that we entrust the supreme command of the armed forces of New Littletown to the nobleman Mishka Toptiginsky. He was the first to point out to us our duty, and he knew how, in a few hours, with forty youngsters and eight officers, to restore order in town and to remove from us the yoke of the Monkey people. I propose that we leave it to him to choose the Chief of Staff, that we quickly take the oath to His Majesty, and that we replace the portrait of King Ludwig XXV—removed by demand of the revolutionaries—with the portrait of His Majesty King Albert IX."

"Hurrah!" shouted the Bears again, and, raising their right paws, they began to repeat the words of the oath that the Mayor was solemnly reading. After that, ovations were staged for Mishka. A formal document, declaring Mishka the Voyevod* of all the armed forces of New Littletown, was drawn up and presented to Mishka on behalf of the Bear populace of New Littletown. Then the crowds dispersed homeward with loud shouts of "Hurrah!" "*Vive le roi!*" "Long live King Albert IX!" "Long live Mishka Toptiginsky!" "Bravo Mayor!" "Bravo Elder Bear!"

Mishka, dead tired, invited the Mayor and Elder Bear to his room above the shop to decide how to run the city in view of the Governor's refusal to continue in his job. It was also necessary to put together appropriate staff and rules for conscription of the populace. Mishka was so tired that his guests had him put on his bathrobe and sit down in the only armchair. The meeting did not come to an end until close to five o'clock in the morning, when the poor little bear crawled to his bed and fell dead asleep.

* Military commander.

The following resolution was worked out during the night at the meeting of Mishka, the Mayor, and Elder Bear. It was submitted to the Town Council and signed immediately.

In view of the difficult times being experienced by our Fatherland, all males from the ages of fifteen to fifty, inclusive, are being called to the colors. The Voyevod's staff will consist of the chief of staff, Lieutenant Colonel (Retired) Prince Leo von Lionburg of the Mishkoslavian army; unranked Mishka Curmudgeon fulfilling the duties of quartermaster general; and unranked Toozik Jolly acting as the personal adjutant of the Voyevod. Internal administration will remain as it was before the revolution, with the administration of the provinces entrusted temporarily to Court Councillor Makitka Crosseyes, and the office of mayor, with its rights and duties, to Mishuk von Berenburg. Only those individuals indispensable to the proper operation of internal government, in keeping with the orders of Mr. Crosseyes, are exempted from the call-up. Families unable to feed themselves in the event of the conscription of the family breadwinner will be put in the town's charge.

    Signed:

Voyevod Mishka Toptiginsky

Mayor and Court Councillor Makitka Crosseyes

Mishka Curmudgeon

    By resolution of the Town Council, signed and countersigned in the name of all the people, by the Acting Mayor, and Titular Councillor Mishuk von Berenburg.

    5 April of the year 1917   Town of New Littletown

The Prince von Lionburg mentioned in the document was one of the participants in the revolution of 1895. He had, however, succeeded in escaping from the Monkeys and had served in the Mishkoslavian army until he ultimately lost his health and became a total invalid. He was forced to lie low in exile until finally a general amnesty, granted by Ludwig XXV upon his accession to the throne, made it possible for the Prince to return home. There he withdrew to his small farm and hardly ever appeared in public. Now he became Mishka's ardent supporter, swore the oath to Albert IX, and with enthusiasm undertook the mission offered him.

The whole population took up arms. Postmaster Swinekin, who was dismissed from his job by the Mayor, was so hurt he immediately sent in his resignation and volunteered. Mishka and Prince von Lionburg visited the drilling grounds in person every day. Mishka, although he was pleased with his success, despaired over the scruffy appearance of the citizenry and over the fact that he could not swear with abandon at some town father or other during the drilling exercises. It also seemed to him that he had insufficient authority. Deciding that as matters stood things would not work out, he seized upon a new plan.

CHAPTER XII

As was his habit, Pushok Pushkovich Junior—the elder son of Councillor of State Pushok Pushkovich Toptiginsky, Consul for the Monkeys to the Eskimo Husky colonies in Africa—picked up the newspaper after lunch. He was preparing for a diplomatic career and therefore considered this pastime his sacred duty. His father was peacefully smoking a cigar. His mother and sisters were busy with needlework. The heat was unbearable. Pushok Senior was on the point of closing his eyes, intending to doze, when Pushok Junior shouted: "Papa! Just listen to this!"

"What?" the father responded languidly.

Pushok Junior, very excited, began to read:

"Paris. April 19. It is being reported to us that in New Littletown a counterrevolution has flared up under the leadership of some kind of twelve-year-old Mishka Toptiginsky. The insurgents have arrested the Commissar and have carried out a series of raids in which a large number of wives of former policemen and of gendarmes and other shady characters took part.

"The Commissar of the 'Transitory Government' drove out to the scene of the disorders. The arrival of the Commissar made a huge impression upon the populace. The punitive detachment that had been dispatched, when it made contact with the forward units of the counterrevolutionaries, retreated, not wanting to spill blood to no purpose, given the strong inclination of the counterrevolutionaries to surrender.

"A series of attempts have been made on the life of the young Toptiginsky, the self-proclaimed 'Voyevod.' He is guarded day and night by his gang. An end to the conflict is expected any day now. Mishka will be handed over to the revolutionaries, who have decided to pardon the populace but to hang the initiator of the revolt to set an example.

"What is most upsetting of all is that Mishka's father, according to rumors, is still in the service of the Monkeys."

Mishka's mother began to sob. Pushok Senior jumped up in agitation and with tears in his eyes cried out: "What a joy it is for a father to learn that his son has become a great hero. What a double tragedy it is for me to lose a son when I only now have fully realized his true nature—without even first having seen him."

Pushok Junior said only: "And I always thought he was such a fool."

When the news was confirmed that very evening, Pushok Senior was fired from his job. But within a day he accepted a position as Consul for Mishkoslavia in that same colony. Pushok Junior took the post of secretary to his father.

But let us not mourn our hero too soon, since we don't trust newspaper gossip. Better, let us see for ourselves what really happened to Mishka.

Part II

LIEUTENANT
TOPTIGINSKY

CHAPTER XIII

And so we have decided to verify the newspaper gossip which, if you might be so kind as to remember, was carried in the newspaper under the dateline of April 19, 1917. We ourselves, insofar as I remember, left our young hero after the fifth of April, the day the famous session of the town council took place, had already passed. And so, on the fifth there was as yet no hint of Mishka Toptiginsky's "tragic situation." However, we shall not accuse the Monkey press of fawning upon the revolutionary government, for we must admit that there were grounds for carrying the report that was published. So, please pay attention.

If you remember, Mishka Toptiginsky, the last time we saw him, was not happy with the authority granted him. As we have said, he had decided that things would not work out as matters stood; so he seized upon a new plan. It is this very plan that is of great interest to us.

Mishka understood well that when the enthusiasm over events had passed, his situation would appear most ridiculous and that, in general, everything that had been achieved thanks to him would seem so amusing and even comic that common sense would take over and the population would reconcile with the "Transitory Government," turn again to its normal business, and toss aside the whole counterrevolutionary farce. So, in order to preserve all that he had won, Mishka conceived this plan: to prolong the general confusion and at the same time to build up so firm a foundation under his own power as well as under his whole enterprise that, when the populace came to its senses, it would be too late and, willy-nilly, they would have to carry through with the matter as begun.

For the realization of his plan, Mishka used the following method. After obtaining written permission from the Governor, he rented the former Governor's Palace. Having bleached the walls and cleaned the floors to remove all traces of the Commissar's stay, he set up in the palace the offices of the Voyevod and of the interim Governor. So many offices were built, with signs on every door, so many stamps and official forms were issued for the Voyevod, Governor, Chief of Staff, Quartermaster General, Adjutant, et cetera, that once the whole town overflowed with forms, stamps, and paraphernalia of various kinds (signs of the Voyevod's power), the populace not only believed seriously in his existence but was even convinced that the Voyevod was indispensable and worked unceasingly.

So that no one would become conscious of what was really going on, Mishka overloaded everybody with work. The Chief of Staff drew up a campaign plan; the Mayor dug morning and night through piles of papers covered with scribbles that the Voyevod had heaped upon him; the Judge investigated the revolutionaries. In a word, everyone was so overwhelmingly busy that there was no time even to consider what the real purpose of the work was. In the Governor's office, Mishka presided solemnly over all this chaos. Unwittingly, everybody soon began to look upon him as some kind of idol, whose stamp or scribbled signature authenticated or settled something.

In the meantime, first having asked the Mayor to set down, as if for a souvenir for Mishka, a detailed description of everything that had taken place, Mishka wrote a deeply moving and touching telegram to the Peace Conference, appealing for help in the name of a dying righteous cause. He attached to his telegram the report of the Mayor, who, of course, had tried to represent Mishka in the most advantageous light. Mishka also sent the Mayor's account to Mishkoslavia to the imprisoned King Albert, writing a very mournful and humble report in which Mishka begged the King to make known his orders. In passing, Mishka expressed the fear that, not finding himself in a legitimate post and not having any real power, he would not be able to accomplish anything. Finally he sent still the same account to Tsar Mishka with a telegram begging the Tsar not to hinder Mishka's dealings with the King—for the sake of preserving the principle of monarchy, a goal with which Tsar Mishka could not but sympathize. To all three, Mishka wrote that he did not feel he had the right to stand witness to his own deeds. He was therefore sending a description of events by a completely unbiased individual who had, moreover, been elected Chairman of National Representatives and whose voice therefore constituted the voice of the people.

While Mishka was awaiting a reply, he continued to throw sand in the eyes of the public; but, so as not to waste time, he studied hard in the quiet of his grand office and passed his exams for four classes, earning a gold medal for his performance.

CHAPTER XIV

Telegrams on Mars, unlike on other planets, take no longer than a few hours, and so, for King Albert, Tsar Mishka, and the Peace Conference, a week was sufficient for the resolution of the situation that had arisen. On the sixteenth of April, Mishka did not go to the Governor's Palace but stayed home for the first time during all this period. In the last week, spring had been advancing by leaps and bounds. Now the leaves were unfurling, and fresh emerald green grass had sprouted in Kadushka's garden. It was a luminous, translucent day, the kind of light, fragrant day when a strange melancholy, some sort of irrepressible longing for something higher, seizes all one's being, when one wants to cry, when one is drawn somewhere and cannot find one's place anywhere. That is how it was with Mishka. On such days he would fall into a kind of especially melancholy poetic mood, and his heart would not be in anything. That is why Mishka stayed home that day in the small room over Kadushka's little shop.

Toward eleven o'clock in the morning, something completely inexplicable happened. Mishka clearly heard drumbeats and loud automobile horns. At that moment, the telephone below jangled. Mishka rushed downstairs, but a frightened Kadushka announced that some sort of foreign officers were waiting outside.

Mishka ran out into the garden. The senior (to all appearances) of the three officers, who were indeed waiting for Mishka, came up to him, greeted him, and said: "I have the honor to present myself—Colonel Count Monte-Gloria du Bolla of the Plumage Ducal Guards." Then he brought forward to Mishka the other two officers and said: "Permit me to present to you Lieutenant Commander Marchese Marini della Aquatori of the Plumage Navy and Captain Viscount Rosaletti of the Plumage Provincial Legions." Finally, having finished with the ceremonial introductions, the Count asked to speak to Mishka in private.

When Mishka had led the officers to his room, Count Monte-Gloria sat down in the armchair that had been offered him and began: "Having learned at the Peace Conference of the disastrous situation and of your heroic conduct, His Highness Plumage XV, the Duke of Plumage, was pleased to send you, under my command, reinforcements now occupying the town, amounting to one mixed corps, numbering five thousand Plumage troops with five hundred pieces of ordnance. Since you are a zealous fighter for world peace, His Highness has sent you the Order of Peace, fourth class." With these words Count Monte-Gloria handed Mishka a leather case containing the order in the shape of a diamond dove on a white moiré ribbon.

"Also," added the Count, "I have the honor to convey to you documents from the Peace Conference, from King Albert and from Tsar Mishka. Besides the papers, I have delivered here one thousand boxes of uniforms from Mishkoslavia and two thousand boxes of arms and cartridges from His Highness."

Mishka took the document sent by the King and read:

With permission of His Imperial Majesty, we are sending you for rapid execution the following orders:

To New Littletown and all its environs, as a reward for faithfulness to their oaths of allegiance and to their precepts of honor, we bestow complete autonomy in domestic and in foreign matters. We declare New Littletown the autonomous Duchy of Neustadt, and we confer upon its capital the name Neustadt. The title Duke of Neustadt is added to the rest of our titles.

We order: the formation of an army and the providing of uniforms, arms, and training in accordance with the orders accompanying our resolutions and decrees.

We order: the formation of His Highness's Regiment of Neustadt Life Guards from the detachment that fought with Mishka Toptiginsky.

Mishka Toptiginsky is promoted to Lieutenant of the Guards and is named Commander in Chief, affording him all the rights of Commander in Chief—including the right to promote to officer rank—and subordinating all civil authority to him.

There is founded the Order of *Pour le Mérite*, fifth class, an order bestowed for outstanding military or civilian service. Individuals of irreproachable and diligent service spanning at least fifteen years are also eligible for the order.

There is founded the Military Order, fourth class, granted for

manifest personal bravery leading to victories affecting the entire course of a war. Both orders are conferred upon the decision of a general assembly of knights of one or the other of the orders and confirmed by the Duke or, in his absence, by the Chairman of the Assembly, that is, the senior knight of the order. We command Lieutenant Toptiginsky to wear the insignia of the order *Pour le Mérite,* fifth class, and the Monkey Order for Bravery, fourth class.

We order the formation of a commission, under the chairmanship of Lieutenant Toptiginsky, to work out legislation for autonomy.

ALBERT

Tsar Mishka sent the newly named Lieutenant a letter, written in his own paw, in which he expressed to Mishka his delight in Mishka's nobility and courage and the deepest regret that the political situation had forced the two to be enemies for a time. To the letter was affixed the Order of Victory, fourth class.

The Peace Conference sent a document in which it recognized all the resolutions enacted by King Albert and declared that it was taking the young duchy under its patronage and protection. Finally, all the European monarchs, for the support of such a brave fighter for monarchy, sent Mishka a present of about 35 million Mishkoslavian rubles from their personal funds and, from government funds, gold worth 1 million rubles as a base for the duchy's treasury.

Words could not describe Mishka's delight; he was beside himself with joy. "But, Count," he exclaimed finally, "how did you ever get by the Monkey army—while you were transporting arms for waging war against it at that?"

"Oh, that was very easy," answered the Count. "We had to bribe only one commissar. The other five were satisfied with a good smack in the snout."

"Well, and now may I invite you to have some lunch? And after that we will go quarter your detachment and look over everything that has been sent to us," said Mishka.

The officers agreed with pleasure and went off to Kadushka's restaurant.

COMPANY GRADE   FIELD GRADE   GENERALS

1. Lieutenant
2. First Lieutenant
3. Captain

4. Major
5. Lieutenant Colonel
6. Colonel

7. Major General
8. Lieutenant General
9. Full General

10. General Field Marshal

Noncommissioned officers bear chevrons on the left sleeve as follows:

Lance Corporal

Junior noncommissioned officer

Senior noncommissioned officer

Ensign

Sergeant Major

Sergeant Major with rank of Ensign

Cockades
Lesser Ranks   Officers

Sword Knots
Lesser Ranks   Officers

General's Plume

Distinctions among various branches of service
The cavalry uniform is distinguishable from the regular uniform by:

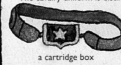

a cartridge box

a fourragère

a pocket on full-dress uniform and cuff on greatcoat

Additional arms of the service are distinguishable by the following insignia on left sleeve:

Infantry Field Artillery Engineer Corps Air Force Transportation Corps Navy Medical Corps Military Police

Order *Pour le Mérite*

5th Class, Officer

4th Class, High Officer

3rd Class, Commander

2nd Class, Vice Chancellor

1st Class, Chancellor

Military Order

4th Class   3rd Class   2nd Class   1st Class

A knight recipient of the 4th class of the Military Order receives the hereditary title of Baronet; of the 3rd class, Baron; of the 2nd class, Viscount; of the 1st class, Count.

Orders of decoration for lesser rankings:

For Service   *For Bravery*

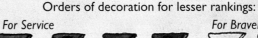

4th Class 3rd Class 2nd Class 1st Class   4th Class 3rd Class 2nd Class 1st Class

After lunch, Lieutenant Mishka, having inspected all that had been sent and after quartering the troops from Plumage in tents in a meadow, called together a secret meeting in the Governor's Palace. Attending were Count Monte-Gloria; Marchese Marini; Viscount Rosaletti; Prince von Lionburg; Mishka Curmudgeon; Bulka Senior, Director of the Neustadt Bank; Mayor Crosseyes; and, as yet unfamiliar to us, Count Fuchs von Ritterschloss, a rich aristocrat who had close ties to many European courts and had been educated at the Imperial Mishkoslavian Lyceum.

Mishka had put on a new uniform, custom-made in Mishkoslavia from measurements sent in a telegram by his tailor. In view of the Commander in Chief's order to put the whole army into full-dress uniform immediately, the Prince and Mishka were forced to pick appropriate full-dress uniforms for themselves. The conference lasted for a very long time, and it was decided to keep the resolutions it passed top secret for the time being.

CHAPTER XVI

Having had real power put in his paws, the young Mishka sharply reversed the way he had been doing things. The palaces, the splendor, the papers—all of them were gone with one wave of his powerful paw—and Mishka turned from words to action. At five o'clock in the morning, on the seventeenth of April, the army was awakened; and, in half an hour, it was brought to combat readiness. At six o'clock, by order of the Commander in Chief, a part of the town was ringed by the army in an impenetrable circle. A second part of the army surrounded the Monkey quarter; and a third part, which had been drawn up in the square by Prince von Lionburg, was read the following brief but significant order:

Carry out a thorough search of the whole quarter and gather all documents and evidence that might point to any criminal activities of the inhabitants. The order is to be fully executed by twelve o'clock in the afternoon. Signed, Lieutenant Toptiginsky, Commander in Chief.

The order was executed to the letter. Postmaster Swinekin tried especially hard. He finally grasped the subtle mysteries of warfare and was even promoted in rank. That very day, for exceptional zeal, he had become a junior noncommissioned officer.

CHAPTER XVII

So now we know what the Monkey press had been referring to as the "counterrevolution" in New Littletown. Now let us see what the newspaper meant by the "huge impression" made by the arrival of the Commissar of the "Transitory Government."

But, first, let us apologize to our readers for the fact that in the last chapter we misled them somewhat when we said that Mishka had forsaken all palaces and luxury. We just wanted to say that he had given up that showy splendor with which he had earlier supported his authority. We can say quite the opposite with regard to his personal life.

In the midst of the wretched houses of the inhabitants of New Littletown, there stood out, in its luxury and magnificence, a palace built at the beginning of the reign of King Ludwig XXV, who intended to spend in it several summer months, an especially pleasant time of year in New Littletown. The environs of New Littletown were a splendid locale for hunting, and King Ludwig, an avid hunter, besides wanting a place for simple relaxation also wanted to make good use of the advantages of the environs of New Littletown for building a royal hunting lodge. With that goal in mind, he built for himself, twenty versts from town, a splendid hunting castle called Schlossburg. However, the hostile attitude of the population of New Littletown poisoned for the King all pleasure of being in the town, and the palace and castle were boarded up and abandoned. In a few years, they were put up for sale. Now Mishka, communicating by telephone with the manager of royal properties, bought the palace, the castle, and all the acreage, for 10 million francs. On the seventeenth of April, Mishka moved into his new abode.

Learning how Mishka had made short shrift of the revolutionaries, the Monkeys flew into a rage. The town closest to Neustadt, Singeville d'Orient, was taken by a corps of revolutionary forces, and a Commissar was sent to Neustadt in the hope that the counterrevolutionaries would hand Mishka over without resistance. However, when the Commissar expressed his wish to enter into negotiations with the soldiers, they immediately sent him to the palace of the Commander in Chief, for which the Commissar was not quite prepared. Nevertheless, when he was led into the small reception room, he tried to gather up his courage and enthusiasm.

In two minutes the door opened, and the Commander in Chief appeared on the threshold. "What do you want?" Mishka asked curtly.

"I come to you, young man, as the representative of the 'Transitory Government,' " the Commissar started to say solemnly.

But Mishka pointed authoritatively to the door and said in a loud voice: "Out!"

"But, young man—"

"Out!" By now, Mishka was shouting.

"But, listen—"

"Out!" yelled Mishka, stamping his foot.

"But—" stammered the Commissar.

"Oh, so that's how it is," said Mishka, and, grabbing the riding crop that was lying on the desk, he fell upon the hapless Commissar, shouting, "Out, out, out!"

Feeling the blows of the crop, the Commissar flew out of the room, thinking only of saving his head. Mishka urged him on from behind, repeating: "Get out, get out, get out!"

And so, again this time, we cannot accuse the Monkey press of toadying. It had not erred in any way. The arrival of the Commissar had, indeed, left a big impression.

CHAPTER XVIII

Let us now analyze the last news item in the Monkey newspaper, and we will see whether it is true that Mishka is in such great danger and how the revolutionaries made contact with Mishka's forces and why and how they retreated.

We have already said that, when the Commissar went off to negotiate with Mishka, there was a corps of Monkey forces in Singeville d'Orient. While the Commissar was busy with negotiations, several more echelons were brought into town, and, on the morning of April 19, twenty thousand Monkeys with one hundred pieces of ordnance set out from Singeville d'Orient. As though nothing were amiss, Mishka went out on horseback to look at the work being done to fortify Neustadt. He was accompanied by Prince von Lionburg, Count Monte-Gloria, and Mishka Curmudgeon, who had been promoted to lieutenant by Mishka when it was reported to him that the Monkeys were three versts from town.

"Are they very drunk?" asked Mishka.

"Dead drunk, Mister Lieutenant, sir," answered the Adjutant, now Lieutenant Toozik Jolly.

"Ah," said Mishka.

"What measures are you ordering taken?" inquired the Prince.

"None," said Mishka.

"For pity's sake! Twenty thousand of them when all we have is five thousand?"

"Do you see, Prince, there on the slope, two squadrons busy training?"

"I see them."

"I will wager thirty pounds of chocolate that I will knock out the Monkeys with those squadrons."

"I accept the bet, Mister Lieutenant! But the business might end up costing us all of Mars," answered von Lionburg angrily.

"Listen, Prince, did you not hear that it's twenty thousand *drunken* revolutionaries approaching?"

"I did hear, and exactly because of that—"

"Excuse me, Prince, for interrupting, but I consider it beneath my dignity to go into battle with drunken ragamuffins. One doesn't fight them, one restrains them; and, for restraining them, two squadrons will be quite enough. Well, and here they are!"

Indeed the Monkeys were appearing from behind the woods. Von Lionburg was furious and, on the sly, was giving orders for drawing up the lines. The Monkeys were approaching in a crowd, without any order, flying red flags. The band was playing something quite outlandish. The "brave warriors" were shouting and making a racket but not at all expecting resistance. When the Monkeys were already approaching the hill on which Mishka was standing, he turned to von Lionburg and said: "Thirty pounds of chocolate!" Then he snatched his saber and yelled: "Whoever isn't afraid of drunken tramps, follow me!" And he rushed alone at a gallop to the bottom of the hill. The squadrons stopped drilling and, with lances drawn, rushed to follow Mishka.

It is well known that drunkards see everything double. For that reason, or from surprise, the drunken crowd took such fright that, without a single shot, they scattered in every direction, throwing down all their guns, arms, and equipment. Up to ten thousand surrendered voluntarily to be taken prisoner. Prince von Lionburg, spotting Mishka, said: "You are a hero, Mr. Lieutenant."

"Only like any mounted policeman, Prince," answered Mishka, smiling politely.

That evening Mishka had guests; they drank chocolate with great appetite. Mishka himself drank so much of it that he almost became ill. Not having wanted to deprive the Prince of 180 rubles, Mishka, that very day, had presented the Prince with a gold goblet worth 300.

CHAPTER XIX

And so we have finished our analysis of the newspaper's report; and, having observed that Mishka's situation was not at all so critical, we can calmly continue our story. The crushing defeat of twenty thousand revolutionary troops left the Monkeys in complete disarray. It is true that, in the time since the revolution began, the Mishkoslavian forces had inflicted more serious defeats upon them, but still, that had happened in a war begun by the King then reigning, and all misfortune could be blamed on the old regime. This latest defeat, however, was dealt the Monkeys by counterrevolutionary compatriots and directed exclusively against the new regime. This was the first serious blow resulting from the revolution.

Street demonstrations and riots began throughout the country. Frightened, the entire cabinet resigned. The Trade Union of Proletarians plundered all the wine cellars.

However, we hope that the readers have not yet forgotten the Major General of the Mishkoslavian General Staff, Mishukovsky, sent by Tsar Mishka to nudge the revolution in a favorable direction. To this "courageous" general belongs not the least important of roles in the story of this stage of the revolution. The General had not been caught napping, and in a short time he was able to bribe so many voices in the Trade Union of Proletarians that he now hoped to install his own candidate as Administrative Minister, a circumstance that would be of great advantage in his further undertakings.

To this end, the General ordered the local plumbing inspector, Simian, notorious for bribe-taking, to appear at his apartment. Simian did not dare disobey the order and was immediately led into the General's reception room. Seeing the corrupt inspector, the General, who was warming himself at the fireplace—the weather in Paris was still very bad—put his paw on a packet of counterfeit five-hundred-franc notes that was lying on the table and said: "Listen carefully, Simian. How would you like to be Administrative Minister? The Trade Union of Proletarians will allocate to you five hundred thousand francs a year in salary. I, for my part, will give you this packet, which contains exactly fifty thousand francs. Besides that, you can take bribes from all your subordinates—which means all the Monkeys, beginning with the ministers. You should be able to rake together a little something that way. A great deal, no?"

"What a deal! What a good deal!" exclaimed Simian, his eyes aglow with happiness as he squinted at the packet of money. "But, Most Radiant Sir, you wouldn't make such a deal for nothing. What percent do you want from me? I am very poor, Radiant Sir. You can't squeeze anything out of me, Your Radiance."

"You are a fool, Simian," said Mishukovsky calmly. "I do not need any percentage from you. The money is all yours. All I ask is that you act strictly in accordance with my instructions. I shall be receiving orders from the Mishkoslavian General Staff. Understood?"

"Yes, indeed, Your Radiance, how happy you have made me! And why should I not obey the Most Radiant Sir? I do not meddle in politics. I am just a poor man. But it's a good deal!"

"So, we have struck a bargain."

"It's done, Your Radiance."

Mishukovsky handed Simian a written contract to sign and gave him fifty thousand francs. That very night, Simian was elected Administrative Minister, and, in accordance with Mishukovsky's instructions, he put together the next cabinet.

CHAPTER XX

Let's look at what our hero was doing during this time. In view of the fact that Neustadt was not sufficiently fortified and could not, therefore, withstand a proper siege, Mishka decided to make an approach to it impossible. Toward this end, he and his troops occupied Singeville d'Orient on the twentieth of April, having first brought the same kind of order to the city as they had to the Monkey quarter. Then they destroyed all the bridges and roads leading to the city, leaving only one highway in case Mishka should want to mount an offensive on Paris. An enemy with the best will in the world would be unable to utilize the highway, since doing so would put him under the crossfire of the Neustadt artillery.

In the meantime, the rumor spread that the revolutionaries wanted to wreak vengeance upon those members of the royal family who were in their power: King Albert VIII (who had been dethroned as feeble-minded); his mother, Queen Cleopatra; and Archduke Karl Ludwig, the brother of King Ludwig XXV. Mishka was horrified and decided that he would abduct all three from Paris. With this goal in mind, to the horror of his compatriots, he changed into splendid civilian dress, got into a marvelous Benz automobile, and, together with Lieutenants Curmudgeon and Jolly and with Mishuk von Berenburg, went off straight to Paris.

General Mishukovsky was pacing around in the dining room, waiting for his tea, when it was reported to him that some young Bear wanted to see him. The General ordered the butler to say that he was not at home. The butler went out. Suddenly the General heard a squeaky voice yelling through the whole residence: "Oh, you old shoe in livery! Do you think, you scarecrow, that you can fool me when your master roars at you in a bass voice that can be heard all over his apartment as though he were beating you with a stick on your blockhead? Go tell General Mishukovsky that, if he won't receive me, he will have to fight me with dueling pistols." There followed the sound of a galosh hitting the butler.

"What a racket out there," thought Mishukovsky. "He calls me 'General.' Hey, my man, let him in," he shouted.

The door opened, and on the threshold appeared a very elegant young Bear. "Excuse me, Your Excellency, but it was lucky for your liveried old toadstool that I didn't break his skull. I have the honor to present myself—Lieutenant Toptiginsky."

Mishukovsky opened his mouth in surprise and exclaimed: "You? Toptiginsky? They will arrest you!"

"Don't worry, Your Excellency. Your minister Mr. Simian, who you thought was taken ill this morning, is sitting in my apartment. It was explained to him, delicately, that if anyone so much as touches me, three bullets will be put in his head. He not only became very meek but even granted me a safe passage. But let's get down to business. I came to prevent a clash with His Imperial Majesty. And it is in your power, Your Excellency, to avert such an encounter. Why are you supporting a republic?"

"Because, if Prince Albert ascends to the throne, war will resume in five years, and we might lose, whereas a republic, with its dissensions, will always be weak, and we shall rule all of Mars."

"Excuse me, Your Excellency, the Monkeys are weak as it is. If you will sign a treaty of alliance with His Majesty King Albert, he will adhere to it scrupulously. And, anyway, you will still have every means of preventing the Monkeys from rising up. Your present policy will be the undoing of all of Mars because you are allowing the revolution to triumph."

"We cannot do otherwise. It is to our greater advantage this way," countered the General.

"Excuse me, Your Excellency, it is not more advantageous for anyone. The example of the revolution is infectious; and, in addition to that, you will have to deal with me, whereas, if you free the King, I shall be your most faithful ally, and I shall choke the Monkeys rather better than you will because I so deeply despise them."

"Excuse me for my frankness and for having put you on the spot, Mister Lieutenant, but measures have been taken against you. The better part of the Monkey forces will be thrown at you. We will take Paris with our bare paws, and from there we shall dictate our terms to all Mars and to you. The plan is infallible."

"Is that the last word, Your Excellency?"

"Yes."

"In that case, I see with regret that I must become your enemy. You bear the responsibility. Your stubbornness is the more useless because King Albert will be freed, and there will be no republic on Mars." So saying, Mishka, bowing low, departed, leaving Mishukovsky dumbfounded.

CHAPTER XXI

Returning to his rented room from Mishukovsky's apartment, Mishka found everything as it was before. Simian, barely breathing, sat in a chair, while around him, in the happiest of moods, sat Berenburg, Toozik Jolly, and Elder Bear, with loaded pistols. "Well, what?" asked Berenburg.

"It's war!" answered Mishka.

"So be it," said all three.

"Well now, my dear Simian," said Mishka, tenderly placing the gun to Simian's forehead, "sit down, and write."

Simian, terrified, sat down at the table. Mishka began to dictate:

"I order passage through all checkpoints without the slightest delay or hindrance for three men disguised as Bears—two adult brown bears and one young white bear—upon presentation by them of this document. Do not impede in any way the departure from the palace of the former King and Queen, and the Archduke Karl; and take all measures so that nobody will suspect the departure of the prisoners. I call upon everyone who holds dear the concept of freedom and of the revolution to carry out this order. According to facts known to me, a plot has been hatched in Paris which perhaps it will no longer be possible to prevent by tomorrow. This matter should be kept in strictest secrecy. The prisoners are to be incarcerated in a distant province. Administrative Minister Simian."

When the paper had been drawn up, the four conspirators went with Simian to his apartment, where the latter stamped the document. After that, the unfortunate minister was driven back to the rented room and locked in a dark closet. Then, when night fell, the conspirators got into the automobile and drove off to the palace.

The order made a terrific impression upon the sentry. The prisoners were awakened most rudely. As soon as they had gotten dressed, they were put in the car by the soldiers themselves. Mishka sat with the prisoners. Berenburg was at the wheel, with Toozik next to him. Elder Bear, armed with the false passport issued by Simian, galloped to the railway station so as to travel through the Duchy of Plumage to Mishkoslavia and there to prepare for the abduction of the King (Albert IX), which our tireless hero had again taken upon himself.

In the automobile, Mishka did not exchange a single word with the prisoners. Berenburg, having driven out past the city, turned off the lights and, with unbelievable speed (ninety to one hundred versts per hour), rolled along the road to Neustadt. Early in the morning, the automobile, covered in dirt, with the horn blowing triumphantly, sped into the enclosure of Schlossburg Castle. The prisoners looked around and didn't believe their eyes. At the castle, the Neustadt and Plumage forces lined the road and greeted the escapees with a thunderous hurrah.

Mishka opened the door, jumped out of the car, helped his honored guests climb out, and, bowing low and kissing the hand of the Queen, said: "Your Majesty, forgive me the unpleasantness you suffered this night, but it was the only way to save you. Henceforth, you are completely free, and my castle and palace in Neustadt are at your service."

The Queen and her son went into hysterics; the aged Archduke Karl tenderly embraced his rescuer and, at Mishka's request, agreed to assist him as a wartime commander. Then, having settled all three in the castle, the indefatigable Mishka got into the car and flew off to Marseilles so that, from there, after buying passage on a ship to Plumage, where he wanted to meet with the Duke, he could go by boat to Mishkoslavia for the abduction of King Albert.

CHAPTER XXII

Meeting with the Duke of Plumage, Mishka secured a promise of help in his difficult undertaking. Although the Duke did not want to be openly involved in this affair, he very much sympathized with Mishka. Even though, to avoid unpleasantness, he had not expressed to Mishkoslavia his indignation at the perfidy involved in the capture of King Albert, the Duke still fully shared the opinion of the European monarchs that the method chosen by the crafty Tsar Mishka to capture his own dangerous enemy was not chosen from among the prettiest.

Armed with the instructions for the envoy from Plumage, Mishka left for Mishkoslavia on the same day. On the fifth of May, he appeared before Count Rivieranti, the Plumage envoy. At that time, Tsar Mishka had come from the front for a rest and was staying with the Tsarevich and his family. The Tsarevich was relaxing similarly on his estate, Little Bullfinch, in the environs of New Mishovka.

Count Rivieranti had rented a nice little villa for himself not far from the Tsarevich's estate. Having received secret instructions to cooperate clandestinely with Lieutenant Toptiginsky in the abduction of the King, he went ceremoniously to Little Bullfinch and invited the entire Imperial Family to his villa, intending to organize several picnics in the vicinity. Tsar Mishka agreed with pleasure and, with his whole family, went off for three days to the envoy's villa. Among the guests was King Albert, who had become good friends with the Imperial Family. He had been staying at the palace in keeping with the rights of an honored guest but with a sentry at his door and at the door of the dwelling because, when Tsar Mishka had asked King Albert to give his word that he would not escape, the King had flatly refused.

It was decided to abduct the King during the night of the eighth of May. Mishka, who was living with the envoy, had managed, while playing the role of a butler serving the King at table, to hand the King the following note:

Go to bed at eleven o'clock. At two climb over the wall at the corner opposite the lake. The sentry will be asleep. Beware of the sentry on the street.

—Toptiginsky

The King became indescribably agitated and suddenly stood up, so pale and nervous that no one was surprised when, complaining of a headache, he went to bed earlier than usual. All the others followed him.

The sentry stood before the King's door in a dark corridor, where Mishka, unobserved, had placed a can of Sleepalia sleeping salts. The salts had such an effect that the sentry fainted away within two hours. All this created so much noise that the Tsarevich ran down from upstairs. Mishka met him on the stairway, profuse in apologies for his clumsiness, thanks to which he had dropped and smashed a vase as he was going to get the gentleman envoy's shoes. As evidence, he showed the Tsarevich the fragments of a vase shattered, indeed, for this occasion.

Then, when everything in the house had quieted down, Mishka changed into field dress, went out into the street, and stood at the prearranged spot most impatiently. At exactly two o'clock, the tall figure of the King appeared behind the fence. Mishka helped him climb over. Things could not have turned out better. Luckily for the King, the sentry was, at that time, on the other side of the house and saw nothing. The King and Mishka went down to the river and boarded a waiting motorboat that was flying the Plumage flag. By morning they had reached Longridge Bay, where a Plumage commercial vessel was waiting to take them to Marseilles. After changing their clothes, they stepped into a car that had been delivered by Berenburg, and on the twelfth of May they safely reached the border of the Duchy of Neustadt.

CHAPTER XXIII

At the frontier of the Duchy of Neustadt, a special house had been designated for the King to rest and change his clothes. During a three-hour stop, the King and Mishka, arrayed in elegant full-dress uniforms and drenched in cologne, fortified themselves with a magnificent snack served with marvelous aged wines. They then climbed into the automobile that had been provided for Mishka and drove past Neustadt straight to Schlossburg. There the King, accepting Mishka's invitation, decided to rest. Driving up to the majestic castle along roads coated with yellow sand, the King was lost in admiration of the magnificent view unfolding before his eyes. Then, turning to Mishka and majestically pointing to the castle, he said: "What a beautiful castle the Duke of Neustadt has!"

"Excuse me, Your Majesty," said Mishka respectfully, with a touch of chagrin in his voice. "Perhaps I acted against the wishes of Your Majesty, and, in such a case, I have the temerity to ask Your Majesty to again take possession of this castle. Up to this moment, it belonged to me, Your Majesty."

"I do not think we understand one another completely," said the King graciously. "I do not at all want to take the castle away from you. And precisely because I knew it was yours, I said that the *Duke* had a splendid castle, *Your Highness*."

At first, Mishka's excitement and joy were so great that he could not utter a word, but, finally, getting hold of himself, he replied: "Your Majesty, I am not deserving of so high a reward."

"Perhaps," said the King. "But your country, having given you to Mars, is worthy of the great honor and happiness of having you as their autocratic and independent monarch, Duke."

CHAPTER XXIV

After arriving at Schlossburg, the King at once put together a plan of action. His return produced a colossal impression. Whole regiments of royalists of the most varied nationalities arrived to protect the King. All of Europe extolled Mishka. The King decorated Mishka with the Military Order, second class, and with the order *Pour le Mérite,* first class, and conferred upon him the rank of Colonel of the Guards. Abundant rewards also rained down on all of Mishka's collaborators. The King formed regiments by nationalities and, joining up with the Neustadt armies, moved on Paris. The revolutionaries sent army after army against him to no avail, and the Mishkoslavians hurried in vain to enter Paris ahead of him and attack him. The offensive of the King and the Duke was a sheer parade of victories. The population, tired of the revolution, greeted its liberators ecstatically. On the first of June 1917, the triumphant procession of the two monarchs ended in their ceremonial entry into Paris.

Part III

HIS HIGHNESS, THE DUKE OF NEUSTADT

The following three odd drawings were intended to accompany a third book on Mishka Toptiginsky, for which we have no text.

Book II

THE RESTORATION OF MONARCHY ON FINCH ISLAND AFTER THE FAILURE OF THE MONKEY REVOLUTION

CHAPTER I

While on morning patrol, part of their regular routine as capitani-reggenti, or heads of state and protectors of Finch Island, Consul Amador-Guererro, Admiral Pardo, and General Porfirio Díaz came upon a disturbing sight. The flag of the Mishkoslavian nation flew over a neighboring island. The sighting could mean only one thing—an invasion of Finch Island by the Mishkoslavian navy was imminent. The three capitani-reggenti knew instantly that their own fleet, composed of one dugout canoe belonging to Admiral Pardo, would be no match for the Mishkoslavian naval forces.

CHAPTER II

CHAPTER II

After a lengthy discussion of the problem, it was decided to submit to the protection of the new conquerors, and Admiral Pardo himself set off in his dugout canoe to talk with the new neighbors. In an hour he returned in sheer delight, loaded with presents for Consul Amador-Guererro and for General Porfirio Díaz as well as for himself. The terms conveyed from the Mishkoslavians were as follows:

· Restore absolute monarchy.
· Give nine one-hundredths of the kingdom's revenues to the Mishkoslavians, and one one-hundredth for the support of the King.
· Include a small Mishkoslavian flag in the corner of the Finch Island flag and communicate with the conquerors in their own language.
· In return for all this, the Mishkoslavians guarantee the Finchlings complete freedom and inviolability.

The conditions were surprisingly good. The Finchlings had been paying one half their revenues to the Monkeys. But, still, such a transition was attended by some danger. Every change provoked a certain discontent in the populace, and the Party for a Republic, strongly supported by the government itself, was very powerful and had a large constituency—numbering up to thirty members. But the interest of the state took precedence over all else in the minds of the three heads of the republic. So the capitani-reggenti decided at once to accept the Bears' protection but to keep everything secret until talks had concluded.

Now what kind of secret can be kept when three individuals are party to it and each individual has a wife? The capitani-reggenti knew the answer better than anyone else. Toward evening, disorders were to be expected (during the day, it was so hot that everyone went to sleep), and General Porfirio Díaz, well in advance, posted army patrols throughout the city and surrounded the houses of the heads of state with a special detachment.

The measures taken by General Porfirio Díaz turned out to be very timely. Part of the population was indeed preparing to stage a noisy demonstration. But it is unlikely that a lazier country than Finch Island exists, and, for that reason, the demonstrators, seeing the patrols, felt such reluctance to enter into any confrontation with them that they postponed their protest.

Life went along as usual, and soon everybody forgot about the future King. General Porfirio Díaz removed his patrols, and, finally, Amador-Guererro was able, without any risk, to call the whole population of the republic to a conference. When all 500 inhabitants were in their places, the Consul said: "Patricians"—the Finchling kings, to avoid friction among the classes, gradually granted everybody the title "patrician," of which the Finchlings were more than a little proud—"I am aware of your anxiety, but surely you do not think that I would let you down when I served for sixteen years as the senior official for the late Don Figueroa X and for four years as the Consul of the Republic. The King will do us no harm, but in making such a compromise, we shall preserve our independence and our wealth. In case of oppression by the new King, our protectors, the Mishkoslavians, known throughout all Mars for their fairness, will defend us against all evil." The Consul received an ovation, and the Finchlings calmed down. Besides, they were too lazy to be upset in such hot weather.

In the meantime, the Mishkoslavians faced a huge problem: Where could they possibly find a black King? But here, too, things soon began to work out. Prime Minister Pig, as he was driving around the park, happened upon a cadet who was as black as a boot. The Prime Minister immediately made inquiries. It turned out that the cadet, Kolobok Medvedsky-Zveroslavsky, was the son of a cavalry captain who had been killed in the war while serving in the Life Guards Regiment of Tsar Mishka I. Kolobok was ten years old. He lived with his mother, Melena, née the Countess of Ebony.

The problem was solved. Melena Medvedskaya-Zveroslavskaya, who very much loved the South, agreed happily to the plan, and so the mother with her son set off for their new country.

Not wanting a ceremonial welcome and knowing the reluctance of the population to restore the monarchy, the young King and his mother traveled to Finch Island incognito, in a launch, under the protection of the Mishkoslavian commandant, Colonel Count Longridge-Mishkin. They were greeted very politely by First Lieutenant Guyon de Matinon-Grimaldi, who suspected nothing and escorted them, at their request, to the King's palace.

CHAPTER IV

Reaching the palace, Kolobok stopped and said to First Lieutenant Guyon de Matinon-Grimaldi: "I thank you for your kindness. But now please see to the raising of the royal standard—because I am your King."

There were no bounds to the surprise and delight of the First Lieutenant. "Well, now, that is splendid, Your Majesty. I will run right now and raise the standard myself," he exclaimed, and he rushed into the inner court of the palace. Soon there stood out sharply against the blue sky a huge white flag with a red-gold coat of arms. In the meantime, Kolobok and his mother set off for the inner rooms in order to transform themselves from modest tourists into the King and the King's mother.

Count Longridge began to walk along the square in front of the palace to be in a position to calm down the Finchlings should any trouble arise. That would be very easy since the only weapons on the island were little knives and rifles and pistols that shot dried peas and small wooden bullets. There were also a few stationary cannons.

The Finch Island population was of a very appealing nature. Seeing the flag that had not been displayed for four years, they were filled with curiosity as to how the new King could have gotten into town without any-one's noticing, and, wondering what he looked like, they ran to the palace. Hearing the noise of the crowd, Kolobok, who had already had time to change his clothes, stepped out on the balcony. Astounded by the brilliance of Kolobok's decorations, the people took off their hats.

"Patricians," said Kolobok, "our great protector, His Majesty Mishka I, Tsar of All the Animals, has entrusted to me the governance of your country. Sadly, I have heard that many of you are unhappy with the restoration of the monarchy. Patricians, we find ourselves in a singular situation. We have been given two options, either monarchy and independence or transformation into an ordinary province. I hope that you will not want the latter. I hope that you will not prevent me from looking after you and governing you and that you will not want to cause our Great Protector any pain."

"Long live Tsar Mishka I! Long live the free Patricians of Finch Island! Long live our new King! Hurrah!" answered Kolobok's new subjects with a friendly shout. From that moment, the King and his subjects took a warm and sincere liking to one another. Throughout the remainder of their lives, they blessed the hour of their coming together.

CHAPTER V

Having in this way achieved union with his subjects, Kolobok officially announced his accession to the throne. Thereupon, in order not to annoy the Finchlings with a foreign name, he took the name Don Rafael III. Then he canceled the Monkey prohibition against civilian clothes for the military and for government functionaries. He kept in place all existing government structures, even leaving Consul Amador-Guererro, Admiral Pardo, and General Porfirio Díaz as capitani-reggenti.

The public was delighted with all Don Rafael's actions. The King himself was no less happy that he did not have to do anything, and he lay around on a rug in the interior courtyard listening to Consul Amador-Guererro explain the mysteries of government administration. Princess Melena (as Don Rafael had ordered his mother called) also liked to lie in the garden listening to First Lieutenant Guyon de Matinon-Grimaldi sing native Finch songs in a pleasant voice to the accompaniment of a guitar.

In general, Lieutenant Guyon de Matinon-Grimaldi soon became a close family friend. As for the lectures of Consul Amador, they served a purpose since Don Rafael was completely confirmed in his decision not to make any changes.

This was the government structure on Finch Island: At the head of the state, as we already know, stood three capitani-reggenti. The Consul was in charge of matters of state. Subordinate to him were the judge, the treasurer, the doctor, the schoolteacher, the postmaster, and a small staff working for the Consul and subordinate to him. Thus government power rested in the paws of Consul Amador-Guererro. Admiral Pardo commanded the fleet. Its makeup we already know. General Porfirio Díaz directed the ground forces, which consisted of twenty-five infantrymen and fifteen cavalrymen, plus three artillerymen and twelve officers.

CHAPTER VI

Don Rafael had been ruling the country for three months. In the Far North, a cold and raw autumn had already set in. But, on Finch Island, nature paid no attention to the calendar. Admiral Pardo and General Porfirio Díaz were lying on the beach with their backs to the sea. They were amusing themselves by tickling each other's whiskers with a piece of wood shaving, having given a name to each whisker beforehand. When one whisker tickled more than another, it signified that its possessor loved very much the individual whose name had been given to that whisker. Of course, it was necessary to purposely pick someone not very attractive; and, indeed, General Porfirio Díaz had demonstrated to Admiral Pardo that the Admiral preferred the young kitchen boy in the kitchen of the Monkey King to the Admiral's own daughter; the Admiral in his turn fixed it so that the General loved the Governor-General's washerwoman more than he liked Don Rafael.

But suddenly their peaceful pursuit was interrupted in a most unexpected way. For a long time, somebody could be heard clumsily slapping the water with oars. However, this circumstance hardly bothered the two protectors of their native land, who were busily occupied. But, finally, the boat moored somewhere quite close by, and suddenly the whole beach resounded with loud grunting, noisy breathing, and the clanging of spurs. There wafted to the keen noses of the capitani-reggenti the aroma of cigars and cologne and the perfume of a marvelous soap.

Both jumped up in fright and saw something to make their hearts sink. General Porfirio Díaz even grabbed his weapon. "My respects," grunted the visitor, and his rich bass voice resounded far over the smooth surface of the bay. "I have the honor to present myself—Mr. Pig, the Mishkoslavian Prime Minister, Adjutant General Aide-de-Camp to His Majesty. Don't worry, I mean you no harm. As for your little knife, my handsome fellow, in view of my corpulence, it could not inflict any significant damage upon me." And the piggy grunted cheerily.

At first, the capitani-reggenti were afraid to breathe, but then, seeing that the apparition was of sweet temper and wanting to get away from him quickly, they bowed courteously, and Admiral Pardo said politely: "We are very flattered by your arrival, General, sir, but we keep very strict order here now; and, for that reason, however regrettable it may be, I am forced to arrest you, even though I hope that the King will order you freed. However, because of existing orders, I am still forced to take this action. Therefore, if you will agree not to escape and will sit here for a while on the beach, we will run over to the King and work out your release." And both high officials, delighted with their resourcefulness, rushed to get away.

The piggy grunted after them: "Fine, fine, kiddies, I will sit awhile," and, grinning good-naturedly, he awkwardly made his way down to the beach.

CHAPTER VII

While Admiral Pardo and General Porfirio Díaz were running to the palace, Mr. Pig, exhausted from the rowing and the sun, sank into a sweet sleep. The appearance of the Premier on Finch Island was not at all so strange as one might imagine. What had happened was that, with the successful conclusion of the war and the celebration of several weddings in the family, the Mishkoslavian Tsar, Mishka I, with his nearest relatives, had set off on a trip to his new possessions and had already been on a neighboring island for some time. That day he had decided to go to Finch Island. Mr. Pig would have made the trip quite comfortably if the young people who teased him persistently had not driven him to make a bet that he could sail across the bay alone.

Half an hour later there arrived the Mishkoslavian Tsar, Mishka I; his son and heir, Tsarevich Mishka, with his wife, Tsarevna Tenderpaws, born a Princess of Plumage; the daughter of Tsar Mishka, Queen Mishuha, with her husband, the King of Shaffkony, Mishuk I; the older brother of King Mishuk, King of the Bruins, Medvedka VIII, with his wife, the sister-in law of Tsar Mishka, Queen Kissa; and the brother-in-law of Tsar Mishka, the brother of Queen Kissa, Grand Duke Purr.

Having had a good laugh over Mr. Pig, everybody began to wake him up. But it was not that easy. The Premier only grunted. Once, when Tsarevich Mishka pulled him by the sleeve, he thought his manservant was waking him and grumbled angrily: "Fool, come back in an hour!" But, finally, the resourceful King of Shaffkony, having found a bit of some kind of grass, began to tickle the Premier's nose. The piggy could not stand that, and he sneezed with all his might. "What's wrong?" he muttered in a hoarse, sleepy voice, rubbing his small, swollen eyes with his chubby little hands. But finally realizing what was going on, he confronted the King of Shaffkony and shouted: "Ah ha! Who won the bet? Hand over ten pounds of chocolate! You miserable tease!"

Still clowning along the beach, the whole group moved off to find the palace of the King, easily enough done since the palace was the only stone building in the whole country.

CHAPTER VIII

Don Rafael, not understanding anything from the reports of his capitani-reggenti, went into deep rapture when his high-ranking guests appeared. Indeed, for him, a plain cadet, to receive in his house the most powerful monarchs on Mars was a great stroke of luck. Tsar Mishka refused all ceremony and spent whole days in the inner courtyard in the company of his wife, Tsaritsa Mishuha, Princess Melena, and the Northland King, Haakon IX. The Finchlings were hugely delighted with the arrival of their High Protector and brought him lots of gold and precious stones to cover the expenses of the war. In gratitude, the Tsar ordered no tribute collected from the Finchlings for five years. He distributed many decorations and granted to the King the Order of the Tsaritsa, first class, for his having been able to deal so well with the people. Thus the Finchlings, their King, and their Protector tied the knots of friendship. Even the most dangerous party, the Party for a Republic, decided to elect Tsar Mishka and Don Rafael as their honorary presidents and provided in the party regulations that henceforth the Mishkoslavian Tsar and the Finchling King were always to be selected for this office. Peace was established on Finch Island for all time.

While the middle-aged animals stayed home, the young ones went hiking, always taking along Mr. Pig, who needed the exercise. It is true that getting the massive minister up the hill was no light task. But the King of Shaffkony and Tsarevich Mishka learned to do it successfully enough, especially since Major Manuel Estrada Cabrera, who had been appointed to accompany the high-ranking visitors, knew the roads very well and always picked the easier pathways. After a good climb, they would rest on some rugged rock where the more settled King Medvedka and his queen would have earlier prepared refreshments.

CHAPTER X

With much pleasure Don Rafael showed the guests all the sights of his domain. Sadly, for him, only Queen Mishuha, Tsarevna Tenderpaws, and Tsaritsa Mishuha's lady-in-waiting, Tenderear, were able to keep up with him. Objects of general admiration were the cannons of light, lacquered wood, which fired cannonballs of the same wood—not so ridiculous in the eyes of the natives as they seemed to the Europeans since those very cannons had protected the Finchlings from an invasion by the inhabitants of the Parrot Archipelago.

In past chapters, we have already talked about how the younger members of the group spent their time. While three of the visitors would be scaling the hills and enjoying the scenery, the fourth would occupy an overlooking promontory to keep an eye on Mr. Pig as he was being pulled along. That was absolutely necessary. The Premier was possessed of a crazy appetite, and anyone who was late to the site of the refreshments risked there being nothing left of the delicious morsels prepared by Queen Kissa.

CHAPTER XI

The days went by so quickly that everyone was surprised to see it was already time to get ready for the return trip. Tsar Mishka was in absolute rapture over his stay on Finch Island. He gave a diamond-studded portrait of himself to Don Rafael; and Tsaritsa Mishuha presented Princess Melena with a coffer full of a variety of jewels. In turn, Don Rafael gave the guests expensive presents from himself and his people. Tsar Mishka, rested and cheerful, promising to come again soon, set off homeward in order to take on with renewed strength his difficult duties as one of the strongest sovereigns on Mars—to whose voice the whole planet listened. Don Rafael personally saw the guests off and waved with his handkerchief for a long time until the three sails disappeared beyond the sandbanks.

CHAPTER XII

Left alone, the Finchlings resumed their regular lives. The capitani-reggenti again got down to business, lying around on the beach for hours, tickling each other's whiskers. As before, the patricians squinted into the sun and praised their King. The King himself lay peacefully in the inner courtyard or went walking accompanied by his mother and stepfather; for, shortly after the departure of Tsar Mishka, a public announcement had been made of the marriage of Princess Melena to Lieutenant Guyon de Matinon-Grimaldi, who had received the title Duke Guyon de Matinon-Grimaldi, Count of Ebony. Peace and quiet again descended upon Finch Island, and one must surmise that this blessed tranquillity lasted for many centuries.

Book III

OTHER PAINTINGS FROM GLEB BOTKIN'S PORTFOLIO

The following watercolors were done by Gleb Botkin in Tsarskoe Selo in 1914, when he was thirteen years old, and in 1915, when he was fifteen years old.
They illustrate popular Russian fables.

"Quartet," by Ivan Krylov
Painted January 3, 1914

"Sharing with a Lion" (author not identified)
Painted January 3, 1914

"The Monkey and the Looking Glass," by Ivan Krylov
Painted September 18, 1915

Not identified
Painted September 19–20, 1915

ABOUT THE CONTRIBUTORS

GLEB BOTKIN was the youngest son of Dr. Eugene S. Botkin, personal physician to the last Russian Imperial Family, and the grandson of Dr. Sergei P. Botkin, "the Father of Russian Medicine" and personal physician to Tsar Alexander II and Tsar Alexander III. The relationship of the Botkin family to the Imperial Family was one of devoted service and intense personal loyalty.

At a very early age Gleb displayed an unusual talent for original drawing and storybook illustration. At the age of nine he began to compose and illustrate his own texts, based on the adventures of animal characters (usually dressed in elaborate uniform), inhabitants of the planet Mars. Gleb's talents came to the attention of Tsar Nicholas II and Empress Alexandra and ultimately captured the interest of the entire Imperial Family, particularly Tsarevich Alexis and Grand Duchesses Marie and Anastasia, who were closest in age to young Gleb.

In 1919, nearly a year after his father, along with the Romanovs, was murdered in Ekaterinburg, Gleb, preparing for his escape from the Bolsheviks, was forced to abandon his albums of animal drawings and stories. These were later returned to him by the friend to whom they had been entrusted.

Gleb Botkin wrote of the Imperial period and the origins of his animal stories in the books *The Real Romanovs* (1931) and *The Woman Who Rose Again* (1937).

Gleb Botkin, who ultimately settled in Charlottesville, Virginia, died in 1969.

Born in Brooklyn, New York, MARINA BOTKIN SCHWEITZER grew up on Long Island. After graduating from Smith College, she married R. Richard Schweitzer, an attorney, and raised a son and a daughter. Mrs. Schweitzer resides in Great Falls, Virginia, and has five grandchildren.

GREG KING is the author of the highly acclaimed *The Last Empress: The Life and Times of Alexandra Feodorovna, Tsarina of Russia* and *The Man Who Killed Rasputin: Prince Felix Youssoupov and the Murder That Helped Bring Down the Russian Empire*. He lives in Everett, Washington.